		- - SEP 2018
6 APR 2019		
2 2 AUG 2019		
2 JUL 2022		

Please return this book on or before the date shown above. To renew go to www.essex.gov.uk/libraries, ring 0345 603 7628 or go to any Essex library.

S

Essex County Council

FOR ISOBEL – HW

FOR YUMAI – BM

First published in Great Britain in
2018 by Simon and Schuster UK Ltd,
A CBS company.

Text copyright © 2018 Harriet Whitehorn
Cover and interior illustrations copyright © 2018 Becka Moor

1 3 5 7 9 10 8 6 4 2

Simon & Schuster UK Ltd
1st Floor, 222 Gray's Inn Road, London WC1X 8HB

www.simonandschuster.co.uk
www.simonandschuster.com.au

Simon & Schuster Australia, Sydney
Simon & Schuster India, New Delhi

A CIP catalogue record for this book is available from the British Library.

PB ISBN 978-1-4711-4722-7
EBook ISBN 978-1-4711-4721-0

Printed in China

This is a story about Violet Remy-Robinson.

Violet lives with her mother, Camille, and her father, Benedict, as well as her cat, Pudding, and her cockatoo, the Maharani. Her home is a flat that backs onto a large communal garden. It is called this because all the people who live in the houses and flats surrounding the garden share it. Violet's special friends who live round the garden are Rose, with whom she also goes to school, and Art, who lives with his great-aunt, an eccentric lady called Dee Dee Derota.

Violet is always on the lookout for adventure and she, Rose and Art have solved four previous crimes: the theft of the Pearl of the Orient, a brooch that belonged to Dee Dee, by the dastardly Count Du Plicitous; the kidnapping of a cockatoo, The Maharani, who now lives with Violet; and, while on summer holiday in Italy, they caught a gang of smugglers. The latest crime they solved was the theft of an Ancient Egyptian mummy from the British Museum.

In all these cases, they had a little help from a policeman called PC Green (very little, Violet would say, although PC Green may say differently) and, when they were solving the case of the missing mummy, they met another police officer named Dolores Jones.

Now, this book, as you might have guessed, features a tiger, so I thought I would begin by introducing the main characters along with their favourite wild animals.

VIOLET

VIOLET HAS DECIDED THAT
ELEPHANTS WERE HER ABSOLUTE
FAVOURITE, ALTHOUGH TIGERS
CAME A CLOSE SECOND.

DEE DEE DEROTA

DEE DEE LOVES HIPPOPOTAMUSES
(OR IS IT HIPPOPOTAMI?) BECAUSE
THEY MAKE HER LAUGH.

DOLORES

DOLORES IS VERY
KEEN ON GIRAFFES

ROSE

ROSE RATHER LIKES ZEBRAS
BECAUSE THEY ARE LIKE
STRIPY HORSES.

ART

ART IS FASCINATED BY WOLVES AND CAN TELL YOU ALL ABOUT THEM IF YOU ASK.

PC GREEN

PC GREEN COULDN'T DECIDE BETWEEN AN ARMADILLO AND A BEAVER.

LADY COMPTON

LADY COMPTON WAS TORN BETWEEN LEOPARDS AND CROCODILES.

This book begins with the popping of a champagne cork and the happy clinking of glasses. It was a warm summer evening in late June and the Remy-Robinsons were having a party.

'Congratulations on your engagement!' Violet, Rose and Art all cried together, grinning at PC Green and Dolores.

WHAT?! I hear you cry. Are you really trying to tell me that lovely, sensible Dolores was going to marry the sweet but rather foolish PC Green? Well yes, that was exactly what was happening. And, as they were SO delighted about it, everyone else was pleased too. Everyone except Dolores's family, that is, but we'll get to that in a minute.

Camille had decided to throw the happy couple a small engagement party to celebrate, inviting Dee Dee, Art, and Rose and her parents. In the end, only Maeve, Rose's mother, had been able to come, as Rose's father and brothers were away for the weekend.

'Well done,' Benedict said, shaking PC Green's hand. 'You must have been amazed when she said yes.' He turned to Dolores.

'Are you really sure about this?'

'Yes, quite sure,' Dolores laughed, bending down to stroke Violet's cat, Pudding, who was being unusually sociable, and weaving between people's legs.

'And we have something else exciting to tell you too,' PC Green said. 'Clever Dolores has won a competition in *Hi!* magazine, and you'll never guess what the prize is!'

'A new fiancé?' Benedict asked, and Camille shot him a look.

'A free wedding and holiday for us and five guests on a tropical island!'

Everyone said things like, 'Wow!' and 'That's amazing!' and 'Lucky you!'

'It's called Tiger Island and it looks stunning. I've brought pictures to show you,' PC Green explained, holding up the magazine. 'The hotel is tiny and the island is really small – there are no cars and you can walk round it in an hour.'

They all looked at the photos and it did indeed look beautiful, with white sand and bright blue sea.

'Are those tree houses?' Art asked.

'Yes,' Dolores replied. 'The hotel has a small

main house with a couple of bedrooms and everyone else sleeps in tree houses.'

'That's so cool,' Art said.

Rose and Violet made agreeing noises.

'The island used to be an animal sanctuary, owned by an eccentric millionaire named Jock Campbell. When he died, he left it to his daughter, who decided to turn it into a hotel, and she has kept some of the animals, including the tiger, apparently.'

'It looks like the most fun place in the world,' Violet said longingly.

'We thought you might feel that way,' PC Green said, smiling at the children. 'So Dolores and I would like you to come too!'

Violet, Art and Rose's mouths fell open at the same time, like a row of baby birds waiting to be fed.

'With Mrs Derota and one of your parents too, if that would be okay?' Dolores asked Camille and Benedict and Maeve. 'I'm sorry we can't have all of you, but our prize is limited to five guests and, as we feel that the children and Mrs Derota brought Percy and I together, we'd really love them to be there.'

Violet was the first to recover from the shock.

'That's so kind of you!' she exclaimed. 'Are you sure?'

'Absolutely,' Dolores replied. 'Percy is an

orphan so he doesn't have any family and mine won't come to the wedding,' she said, looking sad.

'Why on earth not?' Dee Dee cried.

'Because they want me to marry Barry, my old boyfriend,' said Dolores.

'I can see why they might prefer him,' PC Green said, with a sigh. 'He's much richer, cleverer, better-looking and more successful than me, and he's a spy. In fact, he's pretty similar to James Bond.'

'He's not a spy,' Dolores said, smiling. 'His job is to

catch international thieves and con artists.'

'That's exactly what I want to do when I grow up,' Violet said matter-of-factly.

'And I'm sure you will,' Dolores said, and she turned back to PC Green. 'But you mustn't worry about Barry. He doesn't make me laugh like you do, Percy.' She took PC Green's hand. 'Besides, I don't love him.'

'Well, I think you make the most gorgeous couple,' said Dee Dee stoutly. 'And that is a most fabulous invitation. Art and I would be delighted to come if we possibly can. When is the wedding?'

'In a couple of months' time, at the end of August, so it's in the school holidays,' Dolores said. 'And we can all stay for a few days before the wedding and have a nice holiday.'

'We don't have any plans for August so yes, we'll definitely come!' Dee Dee replied. 'Although I'd better sleep in the house - I'm a little old to be climbing up to a tree house. Oh my, a beach wedding! How romantic.'

'That's great news,' PC Green said, high-fiving Art. 'Would you do me the honour of being my best man, Art?'

'Of course,' Art replied and then added, 'as long as I don't have to wear a suit.'

'Nope, it's going to be very casual.'

'Oh, what about a nice little suit with a bow tie? He would look so cute!' Dee Dee said.

Dolores saw Art's face and said quickly, 'Really, shorts and a shirt is fine.'

Dee Dee looked disappointed. 'Of course, it's your wedding, my dear.'

'And I was hoping you two could be my bridesmaids?' Dolores asked Violet and Rose.

The girls beamed and looked hopefully at their mothers.

'That's so sweet of you,' Camille said. 'Of course Violet can come, though I'm afraid I'm away then on a business trip,' she went on, consulting her diary.

Rose looked anxious. 'I would love to go,' she said. 'But can I spare the time?' she asked her mother. 'Don't you think I should be practising for the *École de Danse*? Term begins right after that.'

Now, I need to explain that although Art could carry on in the same school until he was older, sadly the time had come for Violet and Rose to leave their primary school, St Catherine's, and move to senior school. Violet was going on to the senior part of St Catherine's, but Rose had won a scholarship to the top ballet school in Paris, the *École de Danse*. Everyone had made a big fuss of her about it and, although Violet was very proud of Rose, she was also sad that she wouldn't see her during term time.

'It's fine, Rose,' Maeve replied. 'I know I'm

hopeless with dates, but I'm pretty sure that you don't start until the sixth of September, which will give you a few days to practise before you leave. Besides, it will be lovely for you all to have a holiday together. Unfortunately Rose's father will be busy at the office and I'll have to stay and look after Stanley.'

'Do you think you could take a few days off work?' Camille asked Benedict.

Benedict was studying the photos in the magazine intently, particularly focusing on one of a hammock on the beach, with a large multicoloured cocktail beside it.

'I think I could probably arrange some time away,' he replied, a little grandly.

'Well, I think that calls for another toast,' Camille said. 'Please raise your glasses to our future prima ballerina, Rose, to the happy couple, Dolores and Percival, and to a fantastic wedding on Tiger Island!'

And they all clinked glasses again.

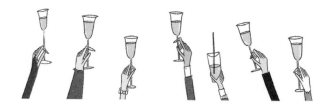

2

TIGER
ISLAND

Let us pass quickly over the next few months, as we all want to get to Tiger Island, don't we? I shall just briefly tell you that Violet and Rose left their primary school, which was a little sad. And Dolores managed to buy some bridesmaids' dresses that both Violet, Rose and Dee Dee liked. As the day of departure drew near, everyone began to feel extremely excited.

They woke up very, very early in the

morning and took a Tube train, a normal train, a big aeroplane, before jumping on a small aeroplane and then finally a speedboat.

You may remember that poor Rose sometimes suffers from seasickness, but this time the water was so calm that she was fine. She found it magical to see the dark shape of the island looming out of the water ahead of her, twinkling with lights like a birthday cake.

And Violet, despite being tired, felt a surge of delight as the boat approached. She could feel the warm breeze on her skin and smell the salty, flowery air.

The boat was driven by a tall, blond young man named Peter, who was the son of the

owner of the hotel and island, Ingrid Campbell. As the boat drew up to the little jetty strung with lights, Ingrid was there to meet them, smiling and welcoming them as she helped everyone off the boat. At first glance, with her short hair and big smile, she reminded Violet of her godmother, Celeste.

'Look at the stars!' Art cried. They all looked up. Above them, the sky was absolutely crammed with thousands of sparkling points.

'Wow!' said Benedict, Violet and PC Green.

'How beautiful!' Dee Dee, Rose and Dolores exclaimed in unison.

'It's because of the lack of light pollution,' Benedict remarked.

'You're absolutely right,' Ingrid replied. 'Because there are no big cities anywhere near here, we see these amazing stars at night.'

A golf buggy was parked on the pier – the only car allowed on the island, Peter joked as he piled their luggage onto it.

'You must all be exhausted,' Ingrid said. 'Let me show you to your tree houses. Peter, please will you take Mrs Derota to her room in the main house and then bring

everyone's luggage?'

It was very dark, except for a few lamps lighting the slatted wooden walkways that criss-crossed the sand. Violet could see bats fluttering through the air above them and the black outlines of coconut palms which gave way to the dark shadows of the jungle beyond. It was all so amazing that Violet was practically fizzing with excitement.

'This is your tree house,' Ingrid said to Benedict and Violet, leading them up a narrow wooden staircase and then along a rope walkway to a little round hut.

Inside was just as Violet had imagined: it had wooden walls and floors, a straw roof and the room was just large enough for two beds, which were draped with mosquito nets. Next door was a smaller tree house, which housed a toilet and a shower. There was no glass in the windows, just views down to the sea and the beach. It was, without doubt, the best bedroom

that Violet had ever seen.

'Ah, here's Peter with your bags,' Ingrid said. 'Can I get you anything to eat or drink?'

Benedict and Violet said no thank you and that they would just go straight to bed.

'Goodnight then,' Ingrid said. 'And see you at breakfast. You can't miss the restaurant. We call it The Shack, and it's on the beach next to the jetty.'

'Well, this all looks very satisfactory,' Benedict said, climbing under the netting and plonking himself on a bed made with plump pillows and lovely crisp white sheets.

'It's just the most brilliant place,' Violet said with a huge yawn, as a wave of tiredness swept over her.

Benedict yawned too. 'Time for bed, I think,' he said and, a few moments later, Violet realised from his gentle snores that her father was asleep. Seconds later, she was too.

Violet slept late the following morning and awoke to sunlight streaming into the tree house, the squawk of parakeets outside the window, and a note by her bed from Benedict which read, 'Gone to breakfast.'

Not wanting to waste a moment, Violet leapt up. She pulled on a pair of shorts and a T-shirt and, after deciding that shoes were not necessary, she careered along the rope

bridge, down the stairs and found herself on a walkway heading for the beach.

Sure enough, next to the jetty was a large wooden platform built out over the sea, with a straw roof and a sign saying

THE SHACK

And there, sitting at one long table, was everyone except Dee Dee and Rose. They all looked very happy with the world and were tucking into a delicious breakfast.

'This place is amazing!' Art said, greeting Violet with a mouthful of banana pancake.

Rose's head appeared from under the table. 'Violet, you have to see these kittens - they're so sweet.' Violet bent down and there, along with everybody's feet, were two tiny, fluffy tabby kittens, fighting over a bit of bacon.

'Oh no, you mustn't quarrel - look there's plenty more,' Rose said, taking a slice of bacon from her plate. 'And there's a tortoise somewhere, apparently,' Rose went on. 'Her

name is Rita, after Ingrid's mother. I think we should try to find her later.'

Violet agreed and helped herself to some breakfast. Dee Dee arrived just as she was tucking into a papaya waffle. With her was another elderly lady, who was wearing a long flowing dress made from pink floaty material, and she had rows of pearls strung about her neck. She was very slight and fragile-looking, and leaned heavily on a walking stick. She looked like a perfect friend for Dee Dee, Violet thought.

'Good morning, everyone,' Dee Dee said. 'This is Lady Clarissa Compton. Like me, she is a little old for scrambling around in tree houses so is staying in the next-door room in the main house.'

Lady Compton said hello, and congratulated Dolores and PC Green.

'Such a lovely place for a wedding!' she said, sitting down with a sigh of relief next to Rose and Dee Dee.

'We feel so lucky,' Dolores said. 'I do hope you'll come.'

'I'd love to. When is it?'

'It's the day after tomorrow, at four o'clock in the afternoon,' Dolores replied.

'Oh! Sadly I have to leave at half past four to catch a flight home, so I will have to miss the party, but I'd be delighted to attend the ceremony.'

'Of course,' PC Green said.

'Thank you. Now, where to start on this magnificent-looking breakfast?' Lady Compton said, surveying the feast.

'Clarissa, this is Rose,' Dee Dee said. 'She is a fantastic ballerina and has won a scholarship to the *École de Danse* in Paris.'

'No, really?' Clarissa replied, looking impressed. 'What a coincidence! I know you'd never think it to look at me now, but I used to be a ballerina with the Royal Ballet Company in Covent Garden.'

Rose gasped. 'It's my absolute dream to dance at Covent Garden!'

'Oh yes, there's nothing like it. I injured my back, unfortunately, and had to give up dancing, but I still love everything to do with ballet. In fact, I always travel with a little statue of a ballerina to remind me of those happy days. You've seen my ballerina, haven't you?' she said to Peter, who had appeared with a tray piled high with even more scrumptious-looking food.

'Yes, it's beautiful,' he said, before wishing Violet and Dee Dee a good morning.

'I show everyone my statue, I'm so proud

of it!' Lady Compton said. 'And are you a ballerina too?' she asked Violet.

'Oh no, not at all,' Violet laughed. 'I'm more of a tomboy. I like climbing trees and exploring.'

'Well, in that case you must look round the island. There's the most beautiful waterfall. You'd better take Peter with you – he can tell you all about the history of the island, and he's handy if you run into Balthazar!'

'Who's Balthazar?' Violet asked.

'Balthazar is our tame tiger,' Peter replied. 'He's a very rare South China tiger; they are practically extinct so he's very precious. He was my grandfather's favourite animal and we couldn't bear to get rid of him, although he does make running the hotel a little complicated.'

Violet's eyes widened with excitement at the thought of meeting a real tiger.

'Is there such a thing as a tame tiger?' Benedict asked.

'That's a very good question,' Peter replied. 'The answer is no, not really, which is why there's a big gate to keep him out of the hotel, and fencing that restricts him to only half of the island and off all the beaches.'

'So can we go and see him?' Violet asked eagerly.

Peter laughed and said, 'He's very shy and often difficult to find. But we can try. Why don't I take you exploring this morning? As well as visiting the waterfall, I can show you Smugglers' Cove. There's a wreck of an old ship there that you can snorkel around if you want? We can take masks and snorkels. Alfred and Enid the turtles live there and they're pretty friendly.'

'Thank you, that would be brilliant!,' Art said eagerly.

'Yes, please!' Violet replied and then glanced at Rose. She was looking worried, partly about running into a tiger, but also about ballet.

'I think perhaps I should be practising my pliés,' she said. 'I've only got a couple of weeks before term begins.'

'Oh, I think the pliés can wait,' Dolores said. 'It's not every day you get to go snorkelling with turtles. You should go and have fun with the others.'

Rose gave a small nod. 'Yes, you're probably right. I can always do some ballet later.'

'Grown-ups are welcome too,' Peter said to the others.

'It sounds amazing, but we need to sort out the arrangements for the wedding with your mother,' PC Green said.

Dee Dee said she was still a little tired from the journey and Benedict said that there was a hammock on the beach with his name on it.

'No problem,' Peter replied. 'Why don't you finish your breakfast?' he said to the children. 'I'll just do a few chores and then we can go.'

3

Gums and Guns

Peter led them towards the gate that opened into the jungle.

'I just need to fetch something from the office before we go,' he said, stopping at the main house. The building reminded Violet of a doll's house, with its balconies and pretty painted wood shutters framing the windows. He explained that Dee Dee and Lady Compton slept on the top floor, while his bedroom and his mother's were on the ground floor, along with the hotel office. Peter disappeared for a few minutes and then came back clutching the unlikely combination of two packets of fruit gums and a small gun.

'Wow!' said Violet, surprised by the gun. 'Is that real?'

'It sure is,' Peter replied.

'That's so cool,' Art said.

But Rose, horrified, stuttered, 'What on earth do you need a gun for? Is it dangerous?'

'No, not at all,' Peter said. 'I always take it just in case Balthazar gets too friendly and then I can fire a couple of warning shots in the air to scare him off.'

Rose looked terrified, so Peter hurriedly added, 'But honestly he's very gentle and shy of strangers. I'll be amazed if we see him at all.'

'I really hope we do,' Violet exclaimed.

'And what are the fruit gums for?' Art asked.

'Those are a treat for Balthazar. He absolutely loves them, especially the blackcurrant ones.'

Violet and Art laughed, but Rose still looked frightened.

'Really, Rose, I promise you, it'll be fine,' Peter said. 'Now, I'm going to take you to Smugglers' Cove first, and you'll be pleased to hear that the path to it is in the half of the island which Balthazar can't get to.' And, slipping the gun and fruit gums into his pocket, he led them through the gate and onto a narrow path.

Violet felt as if she had walked into another world. Everything was green and lush and a bit damp, like an old-fashioned palm house. Above, the trees were full of chirruping birds, and lizards darted across the path in front

of them. As they went, Peter pointed out interesting insects: great hairy orange-and-black caterpillars, enormous butterflies, a nest of black bees in a tree above the path, trails of huge ants marching across the path in front of them and a curious-looking termite hill. They stopped several times to look at the monkeys swinging through the trees and to catch sight of brightly coloured tropical birds.

'You must see these,' Peter said, pointing to a mass of beautiful white flowers. 'They're called Happiness Orchids and are meant to bring good luck.'

Peter also told them a little about the history of the island.

'When my grandfather bought the island, he renamed it Tiger Island. It used to be known as Smugglers' Island, because it was used by a gang of local smugglers to store goods before they took them across to the mainland. That's why the beach here is known as Smugglers' Cove.'

'Were there pirates too?' Art asked eagerly.

'Oh yes, these seas were full of pirates.

When we go to the waterfall, I'll tell you a story about them.'

'And please can we hear about your grandfather?' Rose urged. 'Is it true he had a whole zoo here?'

Peter laughed. 'Pretty much. My grandfather was clever enough to invent a type of widget, which is a crucial part of a machine, known as the Campbell Widget, when he was only twenty-two. It made him a lot of money and, since his passion was not widgets but animals, he and my grandmother bought this island to live on and also as a sanctuary for wild animals who needed a home.'

'How fantastic!' Violet said. 'Did you grow

up here?' she asked.

'No, I grew up in Holland, where my father comes from. My parents divorced when I was a baby, but they're still good friends. We often used to come and visit, and then, after my grandparents died, Mum and I came to live here.'

'You're so lucky!' exclaimed Art.

'Yes, I am,' Peter said. 'But it hasn't been easy. My grandfather had spent almost all his fortune and my mother didn't have the money to keep the island unless we opened a hotel. That meant saying goodbye to a lot of the larger animals, which was tough.

'And running a hotel is fun, but very hard

work since it's just my mother and me. Also it's difficult to make any money at all – it costs so much to bring all the food over from the mainland. My mother is always worried about her finances. And some people come here expecting the hotel to be very luxurious and are annoyed when it's not. Sleeping in tree houses is not for everyone.

'In fact, we've got some people staying at the moment who have done nothing but complain. First, they were furious that we didn't have a swimming pool because they don't like the sea. There are too many fish in it, they said. Then the sand was too hot, then they decided that they had to have breakfast in their rooms, and then . . . I can't remember but there was something else wrong. Now the lady has lost her long gloves and she's blaming me because I can't find them.'

'Isn't it a bit hot for gloves?' Rose asked.

'You would have thought so,' Peter replied with a sigh. 'You can't please everyone, though. Ah, here we are at Smugglers' Cove.'

The vegetation cleared and they found themselves on a small horseshoe-shaped beach, as pretty as a postcard.

'This is where the smugglers used to land their boats,' Peter explained. 'Right, let's get your masks and snorkels on, and then I can show you the wreck. Hopefully Alfred and Enid will be around.'

The turtles were there and the children had a delightful time swimming with them and all the other beautiful fish.

When they had finished swimming, Peter produced one of the packets of sweets from his pocket.

'Fruit gum, anyone?' he said, offering them round.

'Don't we need to keep those for Balthazar?' Rose asked nervously.

'It's fine. We'll save the blackcurrant ones. Shall we go and see the waterfall?' Peter asked.

They made their way back along the same path until they came to a wooden signpost. It read

WATERFALL: 1/2 KILOMETRE

and pointed down a narrow track. They followed this to a high wire fence with a large gate set into it. Peter opened it and then carefully shut it behind them, before leading them onwards.

'Rose, you walk next to me if you're feeling worried, and why don't you take the fruit gums as protection?' Peter suggested. Rose put them in her pocket.

They heard the sound of rushing water before they saw the waterfall, which was about five metres high, with a deep pool below.

'Who
would
like
to slide
down it?
It's   the
best fun to be had on the
island,' Peter said.

'Me!' the children all shouted,
even Rose. It sounded so exciting
that she forgot about being scared of
Balthazar.

Peter took them to the top of the
waterfall, where the stream came rushing
down in a narrow gulley. He showed

them how to lower themselves into the water, which then whooshed them down over the waterfall, to land, shrieking with delight, in the pool below.

As you can imagine, nobody wanted to stop doing that, but, after about an hour, Peter said they should be getting back to the hotel for lunch, so the children reluctantly finished, and sat in the sun, drying off for a few minutes.

'Before we go back, there's something else I can show you,' Peter said. 'But I'd better ask you first if you believe in ghosts.'

The sunny clearing was about the least spooky place you could imagine, but Rose still shivered at the word 'ghost'.

'Absolutely,' she replied.

'Not really,' Violet said, but with a little more doubt in her voice.

Art laughed. 'I don't believe in them at all but I love ghost stories and anything spooky,' he said.

'He's strange like that,' Violet said to Peter.

'Well,' Peter said, 'Art, you'll be excited to hear that this waterfall is meant to be haunted.'

'Who by?' Rose cried, scrambling to her feet. What a morning – tigers and now ghosts!

'A woman and her young daughter, who were killed by pirates two hundred years ago. They had been hiding in the cave behind the waterfall,' Peter replied. 'People say that you can hear them wailing and screaming sometimes, although I never have. My grandmother did several times, apparently. I have to say that the cave is quite spooky.'

'Really?' said Art, his imagination caught. 'Can we go and have a look?'

Rose looked at him as if he was mad.

'Of course,' Peter laughed. 'Do you want to come too?' he asked Violet and Rose.

'NO!' Rose practically shouted.

Violet, as you know, was never one to turn down a challenge, but she knew Rose would hate to be left on her own, so she said to Peter she would give the cave a miss.

'We won't be long,' Peter reassured Rose, before leading Art to the side of the waterfall.

'Follow me,' he instructed as he appeared to walk straight into the waterfall and the rocks behind.

It was like magic. Art followed him through the curtain of water and found himself in a small dark cave. The rock floor was littered with old chairs, boxes, sacks and some rope.

'This was all here when my grandparents discovered the cave, so they left it just as it was. Isn't it amazing?' Peter said, almost shouting over the noise of the waterfall.

'It is,' Art agreed. 'And rather scary, but in a good way.'

'I'm pleased you were brave enough to see it. I think we'd better join the girls now, and get you all back to the hotel. It's nearly lunchtime and I don't want the others to think that Balthazar has eaten us.'

4
UNEXPECTED GUESTS

Much to Violet's disappointment, there was no sign of Balthazar on the way home and the children spent the rest of the day swimming, exploring the hotel and playing cricket on the beach with PC Green, Dolores and Benedict. They found Rita the tortoise, helped Peter feed the chickens and the goats, played with the kittens and generally had the best time. Before they knew it, it was sunset and time to go back to their tree houses to have showers and get ready for dinner.

They all sat at the same long table as they had for breakfast. There was an empty chair next to Dee Dee for Lady Compton, whom they had invited to join them. The Shack looked very pretty, lit with lots of candles and lamps. Everyone was discussing their day and saying how delicious the food on the menu sounded, when suddenly PC Green and Dee Dee, who were facing the entrance, froze.

'Oh my!' Dee Dee gasped.

Everyone turned round to see what they were looking at. Violet was half expecting it to be Balthazar the tiger, but no, it was much scarier. For there, walking in to dinner, were

their old enemies, the Count and Countess Du Plicitous and their daughter, Isabella.

The Count spotted them first, and Violet saw an expression of alarm pass across his face that was quickly replaced with a smile. The Countess and Isabella spied them too, and looked horrified. The Count started to walk towards their table, and the Countess went to grab him. Violet heard her saying, 'No, you must not talk to them!' But the Count shook her off and came over, his smile still in place. He looked, Violet noticed, slightly strange, wearing a bow tie and suit with flip-flops.

'Mrs Derota, PC Green, Benedict, what a delightful surprise,' he said, oozing fake charm. 'And not forgetting dear Violet.' He tried to pat Violet on the head, but she ducked out of the way. 'We live in South America now and have come here on holiday. What brings you to this beautiful island?'

'My wedding,' PC Green replied shortly. 'This is my fiancé, Dolores. Dolores, this is the Count Du Plicitous.'

'Hello,' replied Dolores, looking at the Count with interest. She held out her hand to shake his.

'Congratulations, dear lady, what a pleasure to meet you,' said the Count, taking Dolores's hand and kissing it. 'Now, I must rejoin my wife and daughter. I do so hope you enjoy your dinner.' And he walked back to his table where Violet could see Peter listening politely as the Countess and Isabella complained loudly about the insects, the lack of air conditioning and demanding that they order something different for supper as they didn't really like

to eat the same things as everyone else.

At that moment, Lady Compton walked into the restaurant. The Countess shot up from her seat.

'Oh, Lady Compton, please do join us for dinner. We would be so honoured. Please, I will just get the waiter to bring another chair for you.' She started clicking her fingers at Peter.

'I'm so sorry. I've already promised to have dinner with Mrs Derota and her friends,' Lady Compton said, hurrying away.

The Countess and Isabella looked over at Violet's table furiously.

Violet smirked back.

'Thank goodness you've saved me from having dinner with those awful people,' Lady Compton said under her breath. 'Have you met them?'

'Oh yes,' Dee Dee replied. 'And, let me tell you, they are not only awful but they are crooks. They bought the house above my flat in London, and the Count stole a very valuable brooch of mine. I only got it back thanks to Violet and Rose. And then the family fled the country before the police could bring him to justice.'

'It was terrible that he got away with it,' PC Green said disapprovingly.

'How awful!' Lady Compton said. 'When I

showed him my ballerina statue, he told me he was an art dealer. Oh dear, I hope he's not going to steal any jewellery of mine!' She put her hands protectively over a necklace which had a large sapphire in it. 'It's insured but it was my mother's – I would hate to lose it.'

'I'm sure he won't,' Dolores said reassuringly. 'But you should probably keep your jewellery in the hotel safe when you're not wearing it. Why don't you ask Ingrid after dinner?'

'That's an excellent idea,' Dee Dee said.

'What does it mean if something is insured?' asked Violet, who was always curious about things.

'It means that I pay a bit of money each

month to a company so that if my necklace is stolen, they will replace it,' Lady Compton replied.

Violet nodded, absorbing the information, and thanked Lady Compton for explaining it to her.

'Now, Clarissa, what would you like to eat?' Dee Dee asked. 'I'm torn between the prawn spaghetti and the fresh fish.'

Violet looked over to the Du Plicitouses. The Count and Countess were busy discussing something. Violet and Isabella locked eyes and Isabella stuck out her tongue. Violet stuck out hers right back, until Benedict saw and told her not to.

5

A DISAPPEARING DANCER

Violet slept badly that night. First she was woken by a mosquito buzzing around in her net, then by a noise like a boat engine, and then finally a bird started squawking outside her window at about five. In the end, she got up early and was at breakfast with everyone else when Dee Dee came rushing up, pink and breathless.

'Oh dear, oh dear, can one of you come with me?' she asked.

'Of course, but whatever is the matter?' said Dolores.

'Poor Clarissa is very upset. Her ballerina statue has disappeared. She left it in its usual place by her bed last night, and this morning she woke up and it was gone.'

Everyone looked at each other.

'I hope the Du Plicitouses haven't struck again,' PC Green said.

'Perhaps she's just put it somewhere different and forgotten – could you come and help me look?' Dee Dee replied.

'Of course,' said Dolores, getting to her feet. 'I'll come now. Can one of you find Peter or his mother and send them too?' she asked the others. 'Perhaps with some tea for Lady Compton, if she's upset?'

Rose was already on her feet. 'I've finished breakfast so I'll go,' she said.

'I'll come too,' Art said.

'So will I,' Violet said, keen not to miss anything. She picked up the rest of the pancake she had been eating and shoved it in her mouth in a very unladylike fashion.

'Oh, okay,' PC Green said, watching them go. 'We'd better stay here and check no one steals breakfast,' he joked to Benedict.

'It's the most important role,' Benedict said, pouring them more coffee.

Peter and Ingrid were in the kitchen. When the children told them what had happened, they both looked concerned, but Peter said, 'Maybe she knocked it off her bedside table and it's rolled somewhere. Who would steal it? I can't believe there are any thieves among the hotel guests.'

Violet, Rose and Art exchanged glances, though they stayed silent.

'Anyway, of course I'll come,' Peter said, hastily putting together a tray of tea and toast for Lady Compton.

They arrived a few minutes later to find Lady Compton sitting on her bed, looking

upset, while Dolores searched the room.

'Oh, Peter, someone has stolen my little ballerina,' Lady Compton said.

'I'm afraid it does seem that way,' Dolores agreed, with a sigh. 'I've looked everywhere obvious.'

'Let me just have another look,' Peter said, crawling around on the floor, checking under the bed.

'Nothing else has been taken, has it?' Dolores asked, looking under the curtains again.

'No, I've checked and everything else is here,' Lady Compton replied.

'Well, that's one good thing I suppose,' Dolores replied. 'Was the statue valuable?'

'Yes, very, but thankfully it's insured like my jewellery,' Lady Compton replied matter-of-factly. 'But,' she continued sadly, 'for me it was valuable beyond money – it was the first gift my husband ever gave me. I've treasured it for many years.' And her voice broke a little.

'What an awful thing to happen,' Dee Dee exclaimed.

Violet's eyes began to dart around, but Dolores stopped her with a smile, saying, 'Violet, we're on holiday, remember?' She turned to Peter. 'I think you had better report the theft to the local police.'

He nodded. 'I'll just go and tell my mother and she can telephone them on the mainland,' he replied. 'Then I'll take you and Percival across there in about an hour.'

'We have to go and pick up our marriage licence this morning,' Dolores explained to the others.

Dee Dee nodded. 'You go and finish your breakfast. I'll sit with Clarissa until Peter returns. Now, Clarissa, let me pour you some tea.'

Dolores walked back with Art, Rose and Violet. The three children were already buzzing with suspicions.

'I bet it was the Du Plicitouses,' Violet said.

'They'll definitely have done it,' Art said.

'It does seem likely,' Rose agreed.

'Now, now, you mustn't jump to conclusions,' Dolores said. 'The police will need to look at all the evidence.'

They found PC Green and Benedict still sitting drinking coffee and chatting about football.

'So did the statue turn up under the bed?' Benedict asked.

'Sadly not,' Dolores replied. 'It does appear to have been stolen. Peter's gone to ring the police.'

'Blimey, you don't think that the Du Plicitouses have stolen it, do you?' PC Green asked.

'As I just said to the children, we will have to wait and see what the police think,' Dolores said. 'It's nothing to do with us, thankfully.'

At that moment, Ingrid came over.

'I had no idea that you were a very famous policeman and author,' she said to PC Green.

PC Green tried very hard not to look too pleased and replied, as casually as he could, 'I like to travel incognito.'

'Well, I'm afraid that you haven't succeeded, because the police on the mainland knew all about you staying here for your wedding, and they're big fans,' Ingrid went on. 'Since they're short-staffed and you're such a brilliant detective, they asked if you wouldn't mind investigating the crime yourself. I did explain that you'd be busy most of the day, arranging things for your wedding, but they said that there was no rush and that they can send someone over to pick up any suspects when you've solved the case.'

PC Green looked mildly irritated. 'I was planning to finish my word puzzles and have a long snorkel after we've been across to the mainland,' he complained.

'It's the price you pay for fame,' Benedict said, with a sympathetic smile.

'Poor Clarissa is very upset,' Dolores said. 'It would be nice to try and help her get the statue back.'

PC Green sighed. 'You're right as ever, my love. I'm being selfish.'

'We can help too,' Violet said, feeling extremely excited at the prospect of solving a crime with Art and Rose, especially one where the Du Plicitouses were potentially involved.

Ingrid looked surprised.

'They're very fine young detectives,' PC Green explained. 'We've worked together on several cases. In fact, you could say that they, along with Dolores, are the real brains, not me.'

'I'm sure you are just being modest,' Ingrid said politely.

'I wouldn't be too sure,' Benedict remarked.

'I think that's a great idea, Violet,' Dolores said. 'Why don't you look at the crime scene with Art and Rose, and take a statement from Lady Compton?' she suggested. 'And Ingrid, if we could get the names of the other hotel guests from you, Percy and I can question people before we leave.'

Ingrid replied that of course she could, and they all got to work.

6
THE LIKELY SUSPECTS

Clarissa Compton was sitting with Dee Dee. She still looked very distressed, but had managed to eat her breakfast.

'So,' Violet began, whipping out the pencil and notepad that she had just fetched from her room. 'Please tell me everything that happened, from the beginning.'

'There isn't much to tell,' Lady Compton said. 'Dee Dee and I walked back from dinner together and said goodnight. Then I came into my bedroom, got ready for bed, read a little and fell asleep at around half past twelve.'

'And you didn't see or hear anything suspicious?'

'No,' she said, shaking her head. 'Nothing at all.'

Rose turned to Dee Dee.

'And what about you? Did you see or hear anything strange?'

'I'm afraid not,' Dee Dee replied.

'What did you do after you said goodnight to Lady Compton?'

'Much the same, though I read for a little longer – until about one. Then I fell asleep and

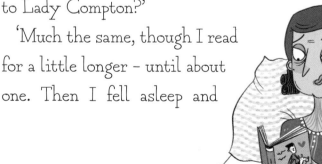

didn't wake up until morning.'

'Okay. Right, if you don't mind, we'll just have a look around.'

Art went straight over to the door to the room.

'Did you lock this last night?' he asked Lady Compton.

'Yes, I locked it with the key, from the inside obviously. It was still locked this morning.'

'Did you remove the key from the lock?'

Art asked.

Lady Compton thought for a moment.

'Yes, I did,' she replied. 'I put it on my bedside table by the statue.'

Art nodded. 'So someone could have unlocked the door and come in that way, if they had another key.'

'You're so clever, Art!' Violet said. 'I'll ask Ingrid who else has a key. What about the balcony doors?' she asked Lady Compton.

'I left them open. It's much too hot to sleep with them shut,' she replied.

'I agree,' Violet said. 'But it would have made it very easy for a thief to get in.'

'Not that easy,' Rose said, peering over the

balcony. 'It's a long way down. I'm sure they would need a ladder to get up this way. I'll go and see if there are signs of one in the sand.' And she trotted off downstairs, reappearing a few minutes later.

'There are some marks in the sand that could be from a ladder, and look what I found.' She held up a pink satin evening glove.

'How very strange!' Violet said. 'Does this belong to either of you?' she asked Dee Dee and Lady Compton.

Dee Dee shook her head, but Clarissa said, 'It looks very similar to the ones that Countess Du Plicitous was wearing the other night.'

'Perhaps it's one of the pair that she told Peter she'd lost,' Rose remarked.

'Our first piece of evidence!' Violet exclaimed.

The only other people staying in the hotel, apart from the Du Plicitouses, were a young French couple with a baby. PC Green and Dolores had finished questioning them by the time Rose, Art and Violet returned to The Shack.

'Could they be suspects?' Violet asked.

'I really don't think so – they seemed genuinely shocked and not suspicious in any way,' PC Green replied. 'What did you think?'

he asked Dolores.

'I agree,' she replied. 'There's nothing to link them to the crime. However, the lady did mention being woken up by a noise at about two that sounded like a motor boat.'

'I heard that too,' Violet said.

'That's interesting,' said Rose. 'Perhaps someone came across from the mainland?'

'Possibly,' Dolores replied. 'But I find it strange that they didn't steal anything else. Did you discover anything useful?'

Violet told them about the glove and the locked door.

'Good work!' PC Green said. 'I think we should talk to Ingrid and Peter next. They're in the kitchen.'

'So you saw and heard nothing unusual?' PC Green said to Ingrid, when they found her.

'No, nothing at all. I finished clearing up around midnight and I was tired, so Peter offered to do the night-check around the hotel. I went back to my room, slept and then I got up at six-thirty and went straight to the kitchen.'

'I see,' PC Green said. 'And what about you?' he asked Peter, who was in the middle of chopping vegetables for lunch.

'I did the night-check and then . . .'

'Sorry to interrupt,' Violet said, 'but what

exactly do you do for the night-check?'

'I walk around the hotel grounds, make sure the main gate is shut, lock the storeroom and the office . . .' He paused and looked worried.

'What's the matter?' Dolores asked.

'I've just remembered that I forgot to lock the office and storeroom last night.' He tutted to himself in irritation. 'I was distracted because I ran into Count Du Plicitous on the way there; we got chatting and then I totally forgot.'

'Count Du Plicitous?!' Five sets of eyebrows shot up.

'What was he doing?' Rose asked.

'He was going for a walk – he said he was

too hot to sleep.'

'And whereabouts did you meet him?' Rose asked.

'Near the main house,' Peter replied. 'I almost ran straight into him because he wasn't carrying a torch.'

'How could he see where he was going?'

Art asked.

'There was a very bright moon last night,' Dolores said. 'What did you talk about?'

'We chatted about the island and the weather – nothing much,' Peter said.

Everyone was silent for a moment, thinking about this, and then Art asked, 'So who would have a key to Lady Compton's room apart from her?'

'There are a couple of spare keys, which we keep in the office,' Ingrid replied. 'It's normally locked at night, but it obviously wasn't last night.'

'So anyone could have walked into the office and found the key?' Dolores asked.

'Yes,' Ingrid admitted.

'Was there any sign this morning of someone having been into the office?' Violet inquired.

Ingrid shook her head.

'None at all,' she replied.

'And do you have a ladder?' Rose asked.

'Yes,' Peter replied. 'It's also kept in the office.'

'Did either of you hear a noise in the night like a speedboat arriving?' Violet asked.

'No,' Ingrid replied.

Peter thought for a moment. 'No, but the emergency generator sounds quite similar to a speedboat. There could have been a power cut in the night and it would have automatically turned on.'

'Is there any way of checking if that happened?' Art asked.

'No, I'm afraid not,' Peter said.

Dolores looked at her watch. 'We really should be leaving now,' she said. 'We'll have to question the Du Plicitouses when we get back this afternoon.'

Dolores and PC Green left with Peter, and Ingrid went off too, leaving the children alone. They decided that they should go and check on Lady Compton and wandered back towards the main house, discussing the case.

'The Count could have easily taken the key from the office, unlocked the door and stolen the statue,' Violet said.

'Or taken the ladder and climbed onto the balcony and got into Lady Compton's room that way,' said Rose.

'Yes, or someone else completely different could have come to the island in the middle of the night and taken the statue,' Art said.

'That's true too,' Violet said. 'But I do agree with Dolores that it seems strange that the thief only appears to have gone to Lady Compton's room and taken the statue but nothing else. Anyway, what do you think we should do now?'

The others were just about to answer when something unexpected happened.

7
A SECRET COMPARTMENT

Ingrid was standing outside the house, talking to the Du Plicitouses. The children walked up as she was saying, 'I'm so sorry you're leaving early.'

'Well, we're not!' the Countess replied rudely with a snorty laugh. 'I am absolutely delighted that a suite has become available at the Grand Luxury Resort on the mainland, especially now the riff-raff have arrived.' She looked pointedly at the children.

'You can't leave,' Violet cried. 'You're our main suspects!'

'What are you talking about, you ridiculous girl?' the Countess spluttered.

Ingrid stepped in, saying, rather nervously, 'I don't know if you are aware, but Lady Compton had a valuable statue stolen last night, and the local police have asked PC Green to investigate the theft. He had to go over to the mainland earlier, but I know he wanted to ask you some questions about it – he's already talked to everyone else in the hotel.'

Violet couldn't resist adding, to the Countess, 'Yes, one of your gloves was found in the sand right below Lady Compton's room, which suggests, perhaps, that the thief threw it away. He or she might have been wearing it to avoid leaving any fingerprints.'

'Why wouldn't they wear both?' the Count asked smoothly. 'It doesn't make sense.'

'Well, we obviously had nothing to do with that as my mother's gloves went missing a few days ago. She reported it to Peter,' Isabella pointed out.

'Yes, she certainly made sure that everyone knew they were missing,' Violet said.

The Countess shot Violet a look. 'I hope you are not accusing me of anything,' she hissed.

'Hush, my love,' the Count said before Violet could reply. 'How upsetting for Lady

Compton. PC Green is most welcome to telephone me later or come to our new hotel and ask us any questions he likes. We have nothing to hide,' he added, before turning to Ingrid. 'The hotel are sending their boat to come and fetch us in fifteen minutes. Please could you bring our luggage to the pier? We've left it outside our tree house.'

'We'll wait in The Shack.' The Countess winced at the word. 'And could you fetch us some fresh pineapple juice?'

'Of course,' said Ingrid.

The Count said a curt goodbye to Violet and the others, while the Countess and Isabella stalked off without a word.

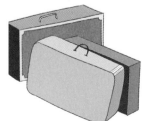

Violet was about to start being rude about them when Rose squeezed her arm and turned to Ingrid.

'Why don't we help you with the luggage?' she said. 'It must be difficult for you to manage without Peter.'

'That's so kind,' Ingrid said. 'But you are meant to be on holiday.'

'No, really, we don't mind,' said Art, who had realised what Rose was up to. 'We like to help. Why don't you go and sort out the juice and we'll get the luggage.'

'But you don't know how to drive the golf buggy,' Ingrid said.

'Oh, I do,' Violet said. 'My father lets me

drive our car off-road so a golf buggy is no problem.' She too had worked out Rose's plan.

Ingrid looked doubtful.

'She's really a very good driver,' Rose confirmed.

Ingrid thought for a moment. The golf buggy was slower than a bicycle so it really wasn't very dangerous and she knew they were sensible children.

'Well, it would be a real help,' she said. 'You will be careful though, won't you?'

'We promise,' Violet said.

'Thank you,' said Ingrid as she handed Violet the key to the golf buggy and explained how to find the Du Plicitouses' tree house.

'Rose, you're brilliant! Now we can search their luggage, and find the statue,' Violet said as they careered along in the golf buggy. They reached the tree house in no time and jumped out, surveying the eight suitcases and bags that the Du Plicitouses had left outside.

'Why don't we start with the three big suitcases?' Rose suggested.

Violet and Art agreed, and they all set to work.

'Remember to look for secret compartments,' Art reminded them.

It was all quite straightforward – the suitcases were unlocked and very neatly packed. But there was no sign of the statue.

'You take these,' Rose said to Violet as they loaded the three suitcases onto the golf buggy. 'And we'll quickly search the other cases.'

Violet drove off with the bags, while Rose and Art checked the rest of the luggage.

'Did you find it?' Violet asked hopefully, when she came back.

'No,' Art replied, with a sigh.

'It wasn't there,' Rose said, sounding disappointed.

'I don't understand,' Violet exclaimed after they had left all the luggage in a tidy pile on the pier. 'Where could the Du Plicitouses have hidden the statue?'

Art was about to say that perhaps they'd

concealed it in their clothes, but then he remembered that the Count had been wearing shorts and a shirt and Isabella and her mother were dressed in skimpy summer dresses with nowhere to hide a statue.

There was a pause before Rose suddenly announced, 'I've just thought of something. What if someone did come in the night, someone who was in league with the Du Plicitouses? They could have taken the statue and be planning to hand it over to them on the mainland.'

'That is possible,' Violet agreed, thinking hard. 'I guess anyone coming to the island would have avoided the jetty, as it's lit at night.

Shall we see if we can spot any sign of a boat landing on the sand anywhere? The tide has been going out all morning so, if we're lucky, any marks made by a boat won't have been washed away.'

Rose and Art nodded vigorously and they set off to investigate.

8

LINES IN THE SAND

The children walked all around the island, scouring the sand for any marks where someone might have pulled a boat up onto the beach. But they found nothing except for driftwood and scuttling crabs. They returned to the hotel very hot and disappointed.

They went for a swim to cool off and then sat under the shade of the coconut trees, drinking mango milkshakes and chatting about the crime.

'Oh well, I think that rules out the thief coming across by boat,' Violet said. 'It must have been the emergency generator that I heard. So do you think that the Du Plicitouses have hidden the statue somewhere on the island?'

After a moment of silence, Art said, 'Do you think that perhaps we're jumping too quickly to the conclusion that the Du Plicitouses did it?'

'They are the obvious culprits,' Violet said. 'Who else could have done it?'

'I don't know,' he said. 'I just think that we should consider whether there's anyone else that we've overlooked.'

Violet paused for a moment, before replying. 'Okay. Why don't we draw up a crime-solving matrix and see if that gives us any other suspects?'

'I'll just go and fetch a pen and paper,' Rose said.

'Right,' she began, when she'd returned. 'Let me fill in all the easy bits. We have no witnesses so let's think about suspects. Obviously we have the Du Plicitouses, but who else could have done it? Dolores and PC Green spoke to the other hotel guests – but there weren't any other possible culprits, were there?'

'No one who seemed at all likely,' Violet replied.

'That just leaves Peter and Ingrid,' Rose replied.

They all thought hard.

'They do have the spare key to Lady Compton's bedroom, and a ladder,'

Art pointed out.

Violet thought that it was somewhat easier to picture Peter climbing up a ladder than the Count.

'But the office wasn't locked, so anybody could have taken the key or the ladder,' added Rose.

'That's true,' Art said. 'Though only Peter and his mother knew where to find them.'

'I think that's a good point, and we should consider making them suspects,' Violet said.

'Yes, Lady Compton had shown Peter the statue as well as the Count,' Rose replied.

'Let's think about motive.'

'Money, surely?' Art said.

CRIME TO SOLVE: THE THEFT
OF LADY COMPTON'S
BALLERINA STATUE

WERE THERE ANY WITNESSES TO THE CRIME?
NO

WHAT CLUES WERE THERE?
A LONG GLOVE BELONGING TO THE COUNTESS
DU PLICITOUS REPORTED MISSING

WHAT CONCLUSIONS CAN BE DRAWN FROM THIS?
NONE FOR DEFINITE

'Well, the Du Plicitouses obviously love money and will steal to get it, but do you remember when we were at the waterfall and Peter said how desperately short of money the hotel was?' Rose said.

ARE THERE ANY SUSPECTS?
THE DU PLICITOUSES, PETER AND INGRID.

DO THEY HAVE A MOTIVE?
YES – MONEY FOR BOTH

DO THEY HAVE AN ALIBI?
NONE OF THEM DO

DOES THIS LEAD YOU TO ANY
SENSIBLE CONCLUSIONS?
THAT WE NEED MORE EVIDENCE!

'I do,' Art replied. 'So they have a motive too.'

Violet considered what the others were saying.

'They seem much too nice, though,' she said.

'Just like Professor Fitzherbert did,' Art said.

Violet remembered how, in the case of the Mummy Mystery, Professor Fitzherbert had seemed so friendly, before they'd discovered what he was really up to.

'You're right,' she said. 'But shall we keep the Du Plicitouses as the main suspects?'

'Yes,' Rose replied. 'I think that's sensible.'

'We should tell Dolores and PC Green when they get back,' Art said.

'Absolutely,' Rose replied. 'Shall we try and investigate first, though, and see if we can find any evidence?'

Violet and Art nodded.

'If Ingrid and Peter did take the statue, it's likely to still be on the island somewhere,' Art said.

The girls nodded.

'The office is the obvious place, or their bedrooms,' Rose said.

'You're right. Let's go and see if the office is empty,' Violet said. But, as they got to their feet, Peter appeared, having just arrived back with Dolores and PC Green. He was clutching a large net and a ball.

'Hi, you three. I hope you've had a good day. Who fancies a

game of beach volleyball?' he asked.

Rose and Violet both looked carefully at his open features, searching for signs that he might not be as nice as he seemed, but Art was too distracted by the thought of playing some sport. He took the other end of the net, chatting excitedly to Peter about where the best spot was to play.

'Perhaps we can subtly ask Peter some questions?' Violet whispered to Rose as they followed the boys. But then Benedict raised himself out of his hammock and joined them, and it seemed too awkward to interrogate Peter.

Hopefully there'll be an opportunity later, Violet thought, but the afternoon slipped away with more games and swimming. They only caught glimpses of PC Green and Dolores, who were busy making wedding preparations, and Ingrid was in and out of her office.

'We'll try and speak to them after supper,' Violet said to Art and Rose, as they all went off to have their showers and get changed.

'I am feeling a little better, thank you,' Lady Compton said, smiling bravely in response to everyone asking her how she was, as she sat down for dinner. 'It was just such a terrible shock and, when you get old, these little pieces of the past mean so much to you.'

'We haven't given up hope of finding the statue,' Dolores said. 'I know the children were hard at work while we were out.'

The children and PC Green and Dolores had managed to have a snatched conversation before dinner, but only about the Du Plicitouses.

'I am determined to catch the thief,' Violet added.

'I'll ring the Du Plicitouses after we've eaten to take a statement and also the local police to see if they have any news,' PC Green said.

'You are very kind,' Lady Compton said.

'Dolores,' a voice called. It was Peter. 'I'm

sorry to interrupt, but there's someone on the phone for you. I think he said his name was Barry?'

'That's strange,' Dolores replied, surprised. 'I'd better go and see what he wants.' And she followed Peter to the hotel office.

PC Green looked rather pale.

'Are you all right?' Rose asked him.

'He's going to try and win her back!' he cried.

'I'm sure it's not that,' Rose replied calmly. 'Don't worry. Look, here she is.'

'You're not going to believe it, but Barry's over on the mainland for work,' Dolores told them as she sat down. 'He's asked to see me in the morning. He was very mysterious and wouldn't say more on the telephone, other than it's extremely urgent and to do with a case he's investigating.'

'Do you have to go? That's right before the wedding!' PC Green exclaimed.

'It'll be fine – there's plenty of time. The wedding's not until four, and he has his own speedboat so he can pick me up and drop me back in plenty of time,' Dolores said reassuringly.

PC Green made a face and said, 'How typical of Barry to have his own speedboat.'

After dinner, PC Green made his phone calls, but neither helped move the case along. The local police had no further information and of course the Du Plicitouses insisted they had nothing to do with the crime.

Lady Compton looked concerned. 'Oh dear! I think I'd better let my insurance company know about the theft.'

'That would probably be wise,' Dolores said. 'But why don't I go and interview the Du Plicitouses again, in person, tomorrow morning and search their rooms? I can easily get Barry to take me to their hotel.'

'That sounds like a good idea as long as it's not going to delay you too much,' PC Green said.

'Yes, you mustn't be late for your own

wedding, my dear,' Lady Compton said. 'Now, let's focus on more cheerful things. Tell me, Dolores, how did Percival propose to you?'

While the grown-ups chatted, Rose, Violet and Art went and sat on the jetty.

'We'd better try to look in the office in the morning,' Violet said.

'Aren't we going on a boat trip?' Art said. Peter had offered to take PC Green, Benedict and the children out to a reef so Dolores could get ready in peace.

'Of course. I'd forgotten,' Violet replied, with a tut of annoyance.

'That's so irritating,' Rose said. 'And we have to leave the day after the wedding so it's our last chance to investigate.'

'I think one of us should stay behind,' Art said, and the other two nodded. 'Let's draw straws – it's the fairest way.' The others agreed, so he ran to the bar, returning a moment later with three straws, one of which he'd cut much shorter. He mixed them up and then, with the lengths hidden in his hand, he held them out for the girls to draw.

Rose went first. She pulled a straw out – it was full length. 'Not me then,' she said.

Violet went next. She chose her straw and drew it out – it was the cut one.

'So it's me,' she said, with a mixture of slight sadness to

miss the boat trip mixed with the excitement of investigating, because that is what Violet loved to do best. Art, on the other hand, was relieved as he couldn't wait to go out on the boat.

'There you are,' a voice said, and Dee Dee appeared. 'I wanted to give you all something as I'm bound to forget in the excitement tomorrow. I dried the rose petals from my garden for confetti before we left – I know how Dolores loves flowers. Look, there was just enough for a little bag for each of you. Will you keep them safe and be sure to bring them to the wedding?'

She handed them each a bag tied up with

ribbon, which they put in their pockets. 'Now, I think it's time for bed, don't you?'

The children got to their feet and they wandered back to their tree houses as Dee Dee chattered on.

'I do really need your help tomorrow – I brought four different outfits for the wedding and I simply cannot decide between them. The peach satin is the prettiest, though perhaps a little hot, whereas the magenta silk is cooler, however maybe too formal, although the emerald green jumpsuit is stunning, but . . .'

9
THE CONTESSA

'Poor Violet's got a terrible headache,' Benedict said as he sat down to breakfast with the others. 'She must have had too much sun yesterday.'

Art and Rose exchanged glances.

'She's going to stay here this morning and rest before the wedding.'

'Oh, poor her,' Dee Dee said sympathetically. 'Well, I'll be sure to check on her. I'm helping Ingrid sort out everything for the wedding.'

'That sounds like fun,' Lady Compton said. 'After I've finished my packing, I'll come and help you, if I may?'

'Of course,' said Dee Dee. 'We'd love that. I will miss you when you're gone, Clarissa. It's such a shame you can't stay for the party.'

'I know,' Lady Compton replied. 'I wish I could, but the airline wouldn't let me change my flight. I can't believe that I'll be at home in Bath this time tomorrow. And without my little ballerina,' she said, with a heavy sigh.

Everyone made sympathetic noises just as PC Green walked in, looking rather crumpled and sad.

'Morning,' he said.

'What on earth is the matter?' Dee Dee asked. 'You're not having second thoughts about that wonderful girl, are you?'

'No, of course not. I'm worried she's going to have second thoughts about me, though, after spending the morning with the amazing Barry. He came really early to pick her up in his super-flashy speedboat, looking all tanned and muscly.'

'You have nothing to worry about. Dolores loves you,' Dee Dee said emphatically.

Meanwhile, Violet was lying in bed, feeling very hungry and waiting impatiently for everyone to leave on the boat so that she could get going with her plan which was basically to spy on Ingrid and, when she was busy in the kitchen or The Shack, go and search the office.

At last, Benedict came back from breakfast to say goodbye and to her relief brought her a large plate of food, 'Just in case you feel better later.' Violet nodded weakly, trying to look as ill and pathetic as possible.

'Dee Dee is down by the beach, helping

Ingrid clear up breakfast and get ready for the wedding, so, if you need anything, go and find her. She said that she'd come and check on you later.'

I'd better get a move on then, Violet thought, although she replied, 'Okay, but I'm just going to sleep all morning.'

'That's the best thing, and then I'm sure you'll be fine for the wedding,' Benedict said. He kissed her goodbye and off he went.

Violet sprang out of bed, grabbed a croissant from the plate and watched him walk away. She listened carefully and, sure enough, soon heard the sound of a speedboat leaving the island.

Excellent, she thought as she finished her croissant, pulled on some clothes and crept out of the door.

She decided to just go straight to the office, and if Ingrid was there she would just pretend she wanted some pills for her headache. So she walked as casually as she could up to the office door. It was slightly ajar, and Violet was about to knock on it when she heard a voice inside that made her stop and listen.

'Good afternoon, this is Contessa di Totola,' the voice said in a thick

Italian accent. 'I wanted to confirm my reservation for a suite for eight days.' Violet was mystified. There was no one Italian, let alone a Contessa, staying at the hotel.

'Very good,' the voice went on. 'You will send a car to the airport to pick me up? My flight lands in Frankfurt at eight o'clock tomorrow morning. Thank you so much. *Arrivederci!*' And whoever was using the telephone replaced the receiver with a click. Violet heard them move towards the door, so she swiftly stepped behind it. She was just in the nick of time as the door swung open almost immediately and Lady Clarissa Compton walked out. Violet stayed absolutely still as she watched the old lady make her way up the stairs to her room, striding briskly and not using her stick at all.

That's so strange! Violet thought as she went into the office. She had a quick look for the statue in Ingrid's desk and all the obvious places, but her thoughts were preoccupied with Lady Compton now. *Why was she pretending to be someone else? Why did she use a stick to walk when she clearly didn't need to?* It was very strange behaviour. *Could it have anything to do with the missing ballerina statue?* Violet wondered suspiciously.

There was no trace of the statue in the office and, aware that Dee Dee might come and check on her at any moment, Violet hurried back to her tree house. She was in the nick of time, for she had only just got back into bed when there was a knock on the door and Dee Dee poked her head round.

'How are you feeling, Violet darling?' she asked.

'Much better,' Violet said, deciding that if she was going to switch her investigations to Lady Compton, it would be easier to get up. 'Can I come and help you and Ingrid?'

'Of course! We'd love that, if you're sure you're better?'

'Oh yes,' Violet replied. 'I'm quite sure.'

'Where did Lady Compton grow up?' Violet asked Dee Dee as they were laying tables in The Shack a little while later.

'In a big house near Oxford. She was telling me all about her childhood – it sounded delightful. So different from mine in the East End! And then she lived in a castle in Wales with her husband. How romantic is that? After he died, she moved to Bath.'

'So she's not . . . Italian?'

Dee Dee looked puzzled. 'I don't think so – she seems entirely English to me. Doesn't she to you?'

'Hmm, sort of,' Violet replied.

'Look, here she comes,' said Dee Dee, noticing a figure walking towards The Shack. 'You can ask her yourself.'

'Oh no,' Violet said. 'And please don't mention it, Dee Dee. She may think I'm being rude.'

'Very well, dear.'

Lady Compton walked into the restaurant, leaning on her stick as always.

'I'm all packed,' she announced. 'You must tell me how I can help.'

'Well,' Ingrid said from the top of the ladder, 'it would be lovely if you could pick some flowers. There are some good scissors in the top desk drawer in my office.'

'I'll fetch them,' Violet said quickly, a plan forming in her mind.

'Why, thank you, dear,' Clarissa said with a smile. 'My bad leg is such a bore.'

The office was empty this time. Violet found the scissors easily and then looked at the rows of room keys. She grabbed the spare key to Lady Compton's room and shoved it in her pocket.

10
THE RED SUITCASE

'Here you go,' Violet said, handing the scissors to Lady Compton back in the restaurant. Then she put her hand to her head and grimaced a little.

'Oh dear, my headache has come back,' she said. 'Do you mind if I go to my room for a bit?'

'Why, of course not! Poor you!' Dee Dee replied, while the others made sympathetic noises. 'Why don't you fetch some aspirin from my room? They're on my dressing table,' Dee Dee instructed. 'The door's not locked.'

'Thank you. I will,' Violet replied, thinking how that gave her the perfect excuse to be in the main house. Everything was going beautifully, she thought. And she went straight off, clutching her head for effect.

The key turned easily in the lock, and Violet opened the door of Lady Compton's room slowly, in case it squeaked. Once inside, she left it open just a crack so she could hear if someone was coming. It wasn't a large room, and it only took Violet a few minutes to search it. She found nothing at all and was about to leave when her eye was caught by a small red suitcase sitting on top of the wardrobe. She stood on a chair to fetch it down and carried it over to the bed. But, when she tried to open the suitcase, it was locked.

Drat! Violet thought. Then she remembered Art's trick of opening a lock with a hairpin and looked around the room for one. But there were none. She was about to give up when she spied a paper clip, under the desk. *That'll do!* she thought, pouncing on it. She bent it as Art had showed her and inserted it into the keyhole, easing the lock up until it clicked and sprang open.

After a quick glance out of the window to check there was no one coming, Violet lifted the lid of the suitcase. And she couldn't believe her eyes, for there, sitting on top of a pile of papers, were seven passports. The first was an American one, and Violet opened the back

page to look at the details. The name on it was Marcia Moore, though the photo was of Lady Compton. Bewildered, she opened the next one, which was French. Again there was a photo of Lady Compton, but the name given was Alice Du Bois. Violet flicked through the rest of them – they were all in different names, but each one had a photo of Lady Compton.

But why on earth would she pretend to be all these different people? Violet wondered.

Below the passports were lots of official-looking documents from companies with names like Brighter Future Insurance, Best Be Wise Insurance Company. Violet scanned them, remembering what Lady Compton had explained to her about insurance. She had insured her ballerina statue for a huge amount of money with lots of different insurance companies, which meant, Violet realised, that Lady Compton would get a small fortune now it had been stolen. Then Violet spied a small package at the bottom of the case. It was wrapped in pink satin, which Violet recognised, as soon as she saw it as being the Countess's other missing glove. Violet unwrapped it carefully, knowing what she was likely to find. And there it was – a small bronze statue of a ballerina. It was so pretty that Violet couldn't resist spending a few moments looking at it.

A noise from outside gave Violet a dreadful start. She dived over to the window to see if someone was coming. She held her breath as she saw Lady Compton approaching in the golf buggy, but then she trundled straight past, looking as if she was heading for the jungle.

Where is she off to? Violet wondered as she quickly put everything back and locked the door. She ran down the stairs and back to the restaurant, thinking she could hear a motor boat. Hopefully Dolores was back.

'Weren't you going to lie down?' Ingrid asked her. 'How's your headache?'

'I took one of Dee Dee's pills and it magically went,' Violet said innocently. 'So I thought I'd come back and help.'

'Are you sure?' Dee Dee asked uncertainly.

'Absolutely,' Violet replied. 'Is Dolores back?'

'Yes, you just missed her,' Dee Dee said.

'She wanted to speak to Clarissa urgently so she's followed her into the jungle. Clarissa sweetly offered to pick some of the Happiness Orchids for the wedding,' Ingrid explained.

Ah, that's where she was going, Violet thought.

'Dolores did seem in a strange mood,' Dee Dee went on. 'Barry brought her back and – my goodness – he is a fine-looking man. Very charming too. Oh dear, I do hope she isn't having second thoughts.'

'I'm sure she isn't,' Violet replied, trying to think what excuse she could make to follow them. She must tell Dolores everything so that they could confront Lady Compton before she left. Violet decided the obvious route was the best.

'Oww!' she cried dramatically. 'Oh no, my headache's come back really badly!'

'Violet, for goodness' sake, go and rest properly this time,' Dee Dee instructed. 'You don't want to be feeling unwell for the wedding.'

'You're quite right,' Violet said, trying to look and sound as ill as possible. 'Sorry I can't help any more.' And she went off towards her room. She only stopped to put a sign on the door, before darting around the back of the huts and through the gate into the jungle.

11

A HANDFUL OF CONFETTI

Violet tore along the path towards Smugglers' Cove. Just before the beach there was a sharp corner and Violet careered round it, nearly bumping straight into Dolores and Lady Compton. Lady Compton was brandishing Peter's gun and, quick as a flash, she grabbed Violet with a strong and wiry grip. Her arms that had looked so frail proved to be incredibly strong.

'Don't move or I'll shoot,' she warned. Her

rather grand, ladylike voice had been replaced by an American accent, with a strong New York twang.

Violet nodded, and stayed as still as a statue, while Dolores said hurriedly, 'Please don't hurt Violet. Why don't you just give yourself up? It'll be much better for you in the long run.'

'And much easier for you,' the old lady cackled. 'There's no chance of me giving myself up and I have a flight to catch so we need to get a move on. The question is what to do

with you two,' she said.

'Aah, yes, I've got it,' she announced, after a moment's thought. 'Dolores, you're gonna drive Violet and me in the golf buggy to the waterfall. And, as they say in the movies, any false moves and I'll put a bullet in you.'

Dolores calmly got into the front of the golf buggy, while Lady Compton climbed in the back, still clutching Violet.

'Don't even think about running away, kiddo,' Lady Compton said as she gripped Violet's arm. With her other hand, she held the gun to the back of Dolores's head. 'Right, move it.'

Violet was a bit scared, but tried to think

calmly. *What did she have that she could use as a weapon?* She mentally searched through her pockets. There was nothing in them except the small bag of confetti that Dee Dee had given her last night. *What use was confetti?* And then she had an idea. *Perhaps she could throw a handful of it in Lady Compton's face?*

Yes, that might work, Violet decided, if she picked the right moment. She moved her hand casually towards her pocket, checking to see if Lady Compton noticed. She didn't. Encouraged, Violet put her hand further into her pocket and began to untie the bag of confetti.

'Do you want me to open the gate?' Dolores

asked as they came to the turning to the waterfall.

'Yes, and get a move on,' Lady Compton replied. She was still holding onto Violet, but her attention was focused on Dolores.

Now's my chance, thought Violet, and she grabbed a handful of confetti. But before she could throw it in Lady Compton's face, the old lady noticed Violet moving her hand and she flicked the gun over to her.

'What are you doing?' she barked. 'Show me your other hand!'

'Nothing,' Violet replied and dropped the confetti on the ground, before raising an empty hand.

'Okay,' the old lady replied. 'Stop messing around. And you—' she nodded at Dolores, '—step on it!'

Dolores did as she was told and, a few minutes later, they arrived at the waterfall.

Waving the gun in the air, Lady Compton ordered them out of the buggy, and told them to walk ahead of her, through the waterfall to the cave behind.

Dolores hesitated. Violet could see she was desperate to try and knock the gun out of the old lady's hand. But Lady Compton was too clever for her and she shoved them forward with her walking stick. Once they were in the cave, Clarissa made Dolores tie up Violet, and then, after checking that the knots were good and tight, she secured Dolores.

'There, that should keep you two quiet,' she said. 'It'll be a good long time before anyone thinks of looking for you here, especially when I've told them that you went off to meet your ex-boyfriend, Barry.' She laughed. 'Poor Percival! He is going to be disappointed! How very sad for him, stood up at the altar. And poor Violet, stuck in her room with a terrible headache. So I'll say goodbye, as I've got a flight to catch.' She hopped back through the curtain of water and was gone.

'I'm sorry you've got dragged into all of this,' Dolores said to Violet when they were

alone. 'As you probably guessed, that lady is not really Lady Compton. Her real name is Marcia Moore and she's a fraudster who has cheated insurance companies out of millions by pretending that her art or jewellery has been stolen. Barry's been tracking her for weeks and I stupidly thought I could handle her on my own.'

She paused, then asked, 'But why did you come after me?'

'I overheard her talking in an Italian accent on the phone and calling herself the Contessa di Totola. I was suspicious so I searched her room and I found the statue and all her different passports and insurance documents and I wanted to tell you,' Violet replied.

'Ah, I see. You are clever, Violet. I would never have suspected her if Barry hadn't tipped me off.'

It was cold in the cave and something moved in the corner near Violet, making her jump.

'Don't worry, it's just a lizard,' Dolores said as cheerfully as she could. 'They'll realise you're missing very soon and come looking for us.'

'I wish they'd hurry up,' Violet said, shivering a little in the cool cave air.

12
TERRIBLE CHOICES

Meanwhile, just as Marcia Moore had been tying Dolores up, Peter was tying the boat up on the hotel jetty.

'You're cutting it a bit fine, aren't you?' Ingrid said with a smile when she saw him with PC Green, Benedict, Rose and Art. She glanced at her watch. 'You only have half an hour until the ceremony. The vicar and the photographer from the *Hi!* magazine have both arrived.'

'Ah, it's fine,' Peter replied. 'I thought it was better to keep everyone out of the way. Besides, all anyone has to do is have a quick shower and get dressed.'

'True,' Benedict said. 'And the reef was so amazing that it was hard to tear ourselves away. Now, we're getting changed in your room, aren't we?' he said to Art

'Dolores did come back, didn't she?' PC Green asked Ingrid anxiously. 'From seeing Barry?'

'Of course,' Ingrid replied. 'She went off with Lady Compton some time ago. I haven't seen her, but I'm sure she's getting ready.'

PC Green looked relieved. 'Thank goodness

for that. She won't have run off with Lady Compton,' he joked.

'No, you're quite safe there,' Ingrid laughed. 'Mrs Derota is getting ready too, and Violet was up and about, but then her headache came back badly so she went to her room about half an hour ago. I guess you'd better go and wake her up soon,' she said to Rose.

Rose and Art exchanged glances. They were both eager to find out how Violet had got on.

'Yes, I will and I'll come and find you if there are any, er, urgent issues,' Rose said to Art.

PC Green looked worried again. 'I do hope there aren't any!'

'No, no,' Rose said hurriedly. 'I'm sure everything will be fine,' she said, and headed off towards Violet's hut.

She was nearly there when she found Dee Dee and Lady Compton deep in conversation. Dee Dee looked very worried,

'Oh, Rose!' she cried when she saw her. 'Something terrible has happened. Lady Compton says that Dolores has changed her mind about marrying Percival and has gone off to meet Barry at Smugglers' Cove.'

Rose gasped. 'That's awful! Are you sure?' she asked Lady Compton.

'I'm afraid so,' said Lady Compton. 'I tried to dissuade her, but she was determined. Poor Percival is going to be devastated.'

'Rose, you must go after her!' Dee Dee said suddenly. 'Try to persuade her to stay. If you run, you might just catch her!'

'Oh no, I don't think that's a good idea,' Lady Compton replied quickly. 'I did try everything, I can assure you. And, besides, it's not safe – Balthazar may be around.'

'Oh, that's true,' Dee Dee said. 'I was being foolish. Perhaps we should find Peter, and then . . .'

'Or perhaps we should just tell poor Percival,' Lady Compton said. 'I can't bear the thought of him waiting, his little hopeful face all anxious and then so terribly sad when she doesn't turn up.'

Neither could Rose. She must stop Dolores going. *But should she fetch Violet first, she wondered? But then that would waste precious minutes . . .*

'Don't tell PC Green anything!' she said decisively. 'Balthazar can't get to that part of the island, so it's fine.' And, before Dee Dee or Lady Compton could object, she sprinted off towards the jungle.

Rose ran quickly and it only took her a little over ten minutes to reach Smugglers' Cove. But when she got there the beach was deserted and the waves were calm, with no boat in sight.

'Oh no! I've missed her,' Rose said to herself. 'PC Green is going to be so upset.'

She looked at her watch. It was ten to four. She began to walk dejectedly back to the hotel. She had just come to the path to the waterfall when she saw Violet's trail of confetti.

That's strange, Rose thought, bending down to look at it. *I'm sure that's the confetti Dee Dee gave to me and Art and Violet. How can it have got here? Could Dee Dee have given*

Lady Compton some? she wondered, and then remembered Dee Dee saying that there was just enough for the three of them. Art couldn't have dropped it, so it must have been Violet. *Had Violet's investigations taken her here,* Rose wondered *and, if so, had she dropped the confetti deliberately?*

Rose hesitated, unsure of what to do. She should really go back and tell Dee Dee that Dolores had gone so that someone could break the news to PC Green, but what if Violet needed her? Rose was about to head to the waterfall, but then she remembered Balthazar and, even worse, the ghosts. She gave a big shudder at the thought of either of them.

Perhaps she should go and fetch a grown-up . . .

She hesitated. But then a voice in her head said quite definitely, *Oh, don't be such a coward! Violet might be in trouble.* So, taking a very deep breath, she opened the gate and ran down the path towards the waterfall.

The clearing was empty and quiet. The sun had dropped below the treeline, making it feel like evening, and Rose noticed that the sounds of the jungle were growing louder, a harsher night-time noise. All in all it was pretty spooky and Rose shivered, thinking, *The sooner I get away from here, the better.*

Inside the cave, Dolores suddenly said, 'Look,

I think there's someone out there. Come on, Violet, we need to get their attention!' And they both began to cry for help at the top of their voices.

Well, you can imagine what happened next. Rose heard the voices calling from behind the waterfall and assumed it was the ghosts of the murdered woman and child. All thoughts of Violet shot out of her head and she could only think of getting out of there as quickly as possible. She turned to run, and then who should come lolloping down the path and into the clearing at that moment, but Balthazar.

Rose froze, for tigers are enormous and quite terrifying in the flesh. He looked at her and gave an almighty roar.

'Help! Help!' came the voices from behind the waterfall and poor Rose thought she might faint from fear.

She scrabbled in her pocket for the tube of fruit gums, while thinking that sweets seemed a very unsatisfactory weapon against a tiger.

They were, however, all she had so, with a quivering hand, she pulled out the packet.

Balthazar licked his lips and padded over to her. He certainly didn't look very shy of strangers, Rose thought, as she tried to extract a blackcurrant fruit gum – not easy with a violently

quivering hand – and threw it at the tiger. He gave a roar of delight and pounced on it like a cat would a mouse. But rather than distracting him or getting rid of him, as Rose had hoped, Balthazar now regarded Rose as a source of deliciousness. He came even closer. Rose edged back towards the waterfall as she desperately extracted another blackcurrant sweet and this time tried to throw it over his head. Excited by what he thought was a game, Balthazar stretched up in the air and caught it in his mouth. He gave another loud roar, licked his lips and came even closer. Rose was practically

in the waterfall by now.

'Help! Help!' The spooky voices floated out into the clearing.

Which is more terrifying, a ghost or a tiger? Well, it was a truly dreadful decision for poor Rose to have to make. But, when Balthazar came so close that she could feel his hot, blackcurranty tiger breath on her legs, and his

strange amber eyes were looking at hers with what looked like an expression of pure greed, she decided that at least ghosts weren't likely to eat her. So, throwing the whole packet of fruit gums at him, she turned and half fell, half tripped through the waterfall.

'Rose!' Violet and Dolores cried in unison.

Rose collapsed on the floor of the cave, panting with fear as she simultaneously braced herself to come face to face with the ghosts, while also remembering that tigers rather like water.

'What on earth are you doing here? Who tied you up?' Rose cried when she turned round. 'I thought you'd gone off with Barry!' she said to Dolores.

'That woman – Lady Compton or whatever name she's using – is such an old witch! It was her who tied us up. You must set us free so I can get to Percy before he thinks that I don't want to marry him. Do you know what time it is?' said Dolores frantically.

Rose looked at her watch. 'Quarter past four,' she replied.

'Oh no!' Dolores wailed. 'Hurry, Rose!!'

'Brides are expected to be late,' Violet said, as optimistically as she could.

'Not this late,' Dolores muttered as Rose picked away at the knots.

'I don't understand,' said Rose. 'Why would Lady Compton tie you up?'

'Because she's not really Lady Compton,' Violet explained. 'Her real name is Marcia Moore and her statue was never stolen at all. She just pretended so that she could claim the insurance money for it.'

'No!' Rose exclaimed. 'But, but . . .' She had so many questions that she didn't know which to ask first and the knots were fiendishly difficult to untie. Then she remembered something else.

'Um, there is another slight problem. Balthazar's outside the cave,' she said.

Violet's face lit up, but Dolores replied sarcastically, 'Oh great.'

Meanwhile, PC Green was standing on the beach, looking very dapper in a linen suit and joking nervously with the vicar about how women always kept you waiting. The photographer was idly snapping away, and Benedict and Art, who obviously knew nothing about Lady Compton's tale of Dolores going off with Barry, were beginning to feel just a little concerned about the bride's lateness.

'Art,' Benedict whispered. 'Go and hurry them along.'

Art nodded and went off.

Poor Dee Dee was in a state of high anxiety, wondering if she had made the right decision in not telling PC Green about Dolores and

Barry, and fretting that something had happened to Rose.

Clarissa, or rather more accurately Marcia, was also feeling nervous, but for exactly the opposite reason, in case Dolores did turn up. She looked at her watch. She was due to leave in five minutes. Peter was at that moment fetching the luggage from her room. She allowed herself a small smile. She'd very nearly got away with it. But she was careful to compose her saddest face as she said to Dee Dee, 'Such a tragedy. I can hardly bear to look at poor Percival.'

When Art arrived at Dolores's tree house,

the first thing that struck him was the silence – no noise or chatter spilled out from the windows. He knocked on the door and, when there was no answer, he opened it. His stomach contracted in alarm when he found the room empty and saw Dolores's wedding dress hanging up, all wrapped in plastic. Baffled, he sprinted over to Violet's tree house to see if she and Rose were there. The do not disturb sign was still in place, but Art ignored it and opened the door. There was no one there. *Where are they all?* he asked himself as he ran back to the beach and signalled discreetly to

Benedict that he needed a word with him.

'I'm so sorry, but I need to go now or I'll miss
my plane,' Lady Compton whispered to Dee
Dee. 'I'll just sneak off,' she went on. 'I don't
want to make a fuss.' She gave Dee Dee's arm
a squeeze. 'It was such a pleasure to meet you.
Do keep in touch. I hope we'll meet again
under happier circumstances.'

'Likewise,' Dee Dee smiled at her friend,
and kissed her goodbye, trying to look jolly,
although she felt more and more wretched
as every moment passed. *Where is Rose?*
she thought desperately. As Lady Compton
walked towards the pier, Dee Dee could see

Benedict talking to Art and looking concerned. She decided that she would have to tell him about Dolores.

14
RARE AND PRECIOUS

Violet, Dolores and Rose emerged from the waterfall, ready to face Balthazar. They had agreed that Rose and Violet would distract him while Dolores made a run for it. But, to their great surprise and relief, the clearing was empty, so they sprinted down the path towards the hotel. It can only have taken them about ten minutes, though it felt like it was at least an hour before they charged through the hotel gate. They arrived just as Benedict was

walking up to PC Green with a heavy heart and a serious expression, saying, 'Can I have a word?'

PC Green looked momentarily alarmed, before he turned to see Dolores, Violet and Rose careering down the aisle.

'Oh, Percy, you are still here!' Dolores cried with relief.

'Where else would I be, my love? And er—' he added, looking at her grubby shorts and shirt, '—um . . . perhaps you're taking the casual dress code a little too far?'

Dolores laughed and then she cried, 'Where's Lady Compton?'

'She couldn't stay any longer so she's just

getting on the speedboat with Peter to head off to the mainland,' Dee Dee replied.

'Quick!' Violet yelled and, along with Rose and Dolores, she dashed off to the pier.

'Should we follow them?' Benedict suggested, raising his eyebrows.

Lady Compton, or Marcia Moore as we'd better call her now, was about halfway along the pier, holding Peter's arm for support. He had decided to get her onto the boat first and then load her luggage afterwards.

'Stop! Police!' Dolores cried.

Peter looked very puzzled.

'Oh, how bothersome!' Marcia said, dropping

Peter's arm and calmly pulling a gun out of her handbag. She pointed it at Dolores and the girls, who froze immediately.

Benedict, Art and PC Green stopped on the beach behind them.

'Lady Compton,' PC Green said indignantly. 'Put that gun away before someone gets hurt!'

'Oh, don't be so annoying, you ridiculous man!' she replied. She turned to Peter, gesturing with the gun. 'Go start the engine up.'

Although he was in a state of shock, Peter nodded and did as he was told.

Marcia weighed up in her mind who she thought was least of a threat. 'Violet, Rose, you load my luggage onto the boat and everyone else, down on your knees.' When no one moved, she raised the gun and fired a shot into the air. *Bang!* Everyone instantly dropped to their knees, except for Violet and Rose who scampered forward, picking up a suitcase each.

'Perfect,' Marcia said. 'No one else is to move until the boat has left.' And she stood on the pier, the gun in her hand, watching everyone carefully.

Then something rather surprising happened. You see, Dolores and the girls had been in such a hurry to get back that they had forgotten to shut the hotel gate behind them.

And Balthazar had wandered in. He sauntered down to the beach, sniffing the air for fruit gums.

'Aaaggghhh!!' was the curious sound that PC Green made when he saw the tiger coming towards them. Benedict shifted nervously, Dolores gulped, while Violet and Rose stopped in their tracks. They all watched the tiger pad up to the jetty towards Marcia.

There was a moment when time seemed to stand still and hold its breath, as Marcia

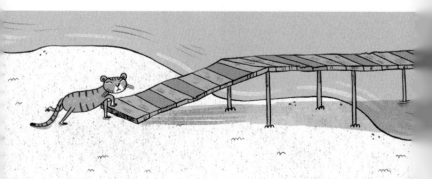

looked at Balthazar and Balthazar stared back at her, as if he was considering her carefully. But then he noticed Rose and gave a roar of delight, recognising her as the human who had given him an entire packet of fruit gums. He bounded over to the girls. Marcia recovered herself and pointed the gun at the tiger.

And then tiger-loving Violet did something very brave. As terrified as she was of being shot or of being eaten by a tiger, she couldn't bear the thought of Balthazar getting hurt.

'NO!!' she shouted at Marcia and, with the suitcase held in front of her like a shield, she ran with all her might at the old lady, who whipped round to fire the gun. As she did so, Violet hurtled into her. The gun went off with a cracking bang, sending a bullet spinning through the air, before it was knocked out of Marcia's hand as she and Violet both tumbled off the jetty and into the water.

Then lots of things happened at once.

Balthazar gave a roar of fright and bounded off towards the jungle.

'OOWWWW!' PC Green cried, clutching his ear. 'I've been shot!'

Dolores and Peter ran over to him.

Art and Rose dived into the water to capture Marcia.

'Oh, you wretched, interfering children,' she cursed as they took hold of her and marched her onto the beach.

Benedict charged into the water to get to Violet, who was standing up, looking slightly bewildered.

'Are you all right?' he cried. 'You mustn't do things like that! You could have been shot.'

'I'm absolutely fine,' she replied matter-of-factly, wiping the water from her eyes. 'I couldn't let her shoot Balthazar. He's very rare and precious.'

Benedict laughed. 'And so are you, Violet, so are you.'

15
A Bit of Soppiness

It's amazing what you can achieve in an hour if you put your mind to it.

The mark on PC Green's ear was pronounced just a scratch and was soon remedied with a cocktail and a bit of first aid. Dolores tried to telephone Barry, but couldn't get hold of him, and she spoke to the local police instead. They decided they weren't so busy and sent a boat immediately to pick up Marcia Moore.

So just an hour later, as the sun was

sinking in the sky, Dolores walked down the sandy aisle again, this time looking rather more glamorous, dressed in a beautiful, flowing white dress. Rose and Violet were behind her, scrubbed and clean in their bridesmaids' dresses.

PC Green grinned from ear to bandaged ear at the sight of them.

Dolores took her place at his side and the vicar started to speak.

'Welcome, everyone. We are here to witness the marriage of Dolores Jones and Percival Green.' He had just got to the bit where he said, 'If any man has any objection to this marriage,' when he was interrupted by the roar of a motor boat pulling into the jetty.

'Oh, what now?' PC Green cried. And, as everyone squinted in the fading light to see who was onboard, he gave a horrified squawk.

'Oh no! It's Barry, with lots of other people. He's come to claim you!' he said to Dolores.

Dolores peered hard. She was silent for a moment and then said, 'But . . . that's my family!' She scanned the party on the boat. 'Mum!' she cried as she spotted a smartly dressed, middle-aged lady climbing onto the jetty. Dolores ran over to her.

'They're staging an intervention!' PC Green said, his voice squeaky with panic. 'I can't bear it . . .' He sank to his knees, looking like he was about to cry.

'Come on! You've got to stand up for yourself!' Violet cried.

'Quite,' said Dee Dee, sounding unusually strict. 'Percival, you're just going to have to fight for Dolores.'

'You're right,' he said, taking a deep breath and standing up, flexing his hands like a boxer preparing for a fight.

'They don't look like they're objecting,' Rose said, watching Dolores start to hug people.

'Perhaps they changed their mind and have come to the wedding?' Benedict said.

PC Green wasn't listening. He was watching Barry, who was walking slowly towards him.

'Blimey, he's a big bloke,' Benedict said, rather unhelpfully.

'Barry, if you want Dolores,' PC Green said, trying to sound as tough as he could and raising his fists, 'you're going to have to kill me first.'

Barry let out a hoot of laughter. 'I'm not here to fight you, Percival,' he said. 'I wanted to congratulate you myself and wish you and Dolores all the happiness in the world.'

PC Green dropped his fists.

'Really, are you sure?' he asked.

'Positive,' replied Barry.

'Well, that's a relief. I didn't fancy my chances against you at all. But then why are all Dolores's family here?' he asked. 'Do they want to fight me?' He looked concerned again.

'No, of course not. I knew how upset Dolores was that they weren't here so I persuaded them to come.'

PC Green looked amazed. 'That's very kind

of you,' he replied.

'I didn't want there to be any hard feelings between us. I know how much Dolores loves you.'

PC Green went all pink and soppy-looking.

'Awww, that's so nice of you, Barry, thank you,' he said, and Barry laughed.

And so, as the sun was setting, Dolores walked down the aisle for the third time, watched by all her family.

'Fingers crossed this time,' Benedict said.

'Shh, it'll be fine,' Violet said, taking her place next to him.

And it was. All was well and PC Green married Inspector Dolores Jones.

The party went on late into the night. Ingrid and Peter worked magic with the food and drink and somehow there was enough for everyone. Violet, Art and Rose helped with the serving and the washing-up, and, when all the work was done, the three friends sat on the beach, gazing up at the stars, with fireflies zipping around them.

Through the darkness they heard a voice say, 'Well, there you lot are! I've been looking for you everywhere. You must try some

of this wedding cake.' PC Green appeared, holding three plates of cake. 'Dolores's mum made it and brought it all the way in her hand luggage. It's completely scrumptious.'

They all began munching. It was absolutely delicious.

'Well, chaps,' said PC Green. 'Another criminal caught, thanks to you lot. You are amazing.'

'Not really. None of us suspected Lady Compton at first,' Rose pointed out.

'She was very clever – there was no evidence linking her to the crime at all,' Art said.

'It's true. The Du Plicitouses did seem like the obvious suspects,' Violet said. 'I do feel slightly bad for accusing them.'

'I know. Perhaps we should write them a letter to apologise?' Rose said earnestly, and the other three laughed.

'No! Don't forget that they got away with stealing Dee Dee's brooch,' PC Green said.

'That's true,' Rose admitted.

'And they are really horrible,' Violet said.

'That's also true,' Rose added.

'But chaps, just think – if it wasn't for Count Du Plicitous, I would never have met you,' PC Green said. 'And nothing would have been the same.'

'That's true too,' Violet replied. 'So, in fact, we have a lot to thank him for.'

They all laughed and then were quiet for a moment, finishing their cake.

'And, er, I wanted to say thanks for everything, you know, for coming to the wedding and being my friends and helping me solve crimes,' PC Green said awkwardly.

They were all about to make various replies when Dee Dee's voice wafted over to them. 'Percival, come and dance!'

'Duty calls,' PC Green said, getting to his feet. 'I'd better go and show them some moves. King of the dance floor, that's me! See you later, chaps.'

'I can't believe that we have to go home tomorrow,' Violet said with a sigh.

'And I'll be in Paris in a week's time,' Rose said, sounding more sad than excited.

'It'll be really fun, I'm sure,' Art said kindly. 'I was nervous before I started my new school, but it didn't take me long to love it there.'

'I'm worried I'm going to be really homesick. I wish I was just going to St Catherine's with you,' she blurted out to Violet.

'I wish you were too,' Violet said, giving Rose a hug. 'But think how wonderful it will be in Paris! You'll have so many adventures.'

'Will you both come and see me?' she asked tentatively.

'Yes!' they cried.

'And we'll all still be friends?' Rose

asked shyly.

'Of course. We'll always be friends,' Violet said. And then, deciding that she was sounding as soppy as PC Green, she sprang to her feet and cried, 'Who's up for a midnight swim?'

'Me!' Art and Rose yelled, and the three of them charged together into the dark blue water.

16
CAROL SINGERS

This book started with a party and ends with one too.

It was the twentieth of December and the Remy-Robinsons' flat was looking delightfully Christmassy. The delicious smell of Norma's yummy mince pies, which she had baked before going home to spend Christmas with her family, wafted through the air, a jolly fire was burning in the grate and the Christmas tree was laden with baubles, candy canes and twinkling lights. The Maharani was perched on the top of it rather than a fairy, and Pudding was lying stretched out in front of the fire, unaware that his peace was about to be shattered.

Violet was sitting on the sofa, helping Grand-mère put the finishing touches to her dog Alphonse's Christmas party outfit, which was a very smart jumper with a pattern of reindeers all over it and some reindeer ears to match. They had all been laughing at the Christmas card that Violet's aunt, Matilde, and her daughter, Agnes had sent of them, of Mr Ratty, Agnes's pet rat, dressed up as Father Christmas.

'Now, chérie, when is Rose back?' Grand-mère asked.

'Not until the day after tomorrow,' Violet said with a sigh. It had been a long separation and, although they wrote to each other every week, it was not the same as being together.

'Such a shame that she's missing the party,' Grand-mère said. Then, seeing Violet's sad face, she said quickly, 'But you must be so pleased about your detective summer school next year.'

Violet immediately perked up.

'I can't wait,' she replied excitedly. Barry had put her forward for a course run by the police and, although she was technically too young for it, they had been so impressed with her crime-solving abilities that they had bent the rules for her.

Brinngg! went the doorbell.

'Ah, guests!' Camille said, coming in from the kitchen. 'Please will you answer the door, Violet?'

Uncle Johnny and Elena were the first to arrive, with their baby Lucia. She had just started to walk and Violet secretly thought she looked a bit like Frankenstein's monster when she staggered around with her arms straight out in front of her. Lucia loved Pudding and she started to cry, 'DAT!!! DAT!!!' and charged towards him. Horrified, Pudding darted off

to hide in Violet's bedroom.

'Never mind,' Elena said, scooping up Lucia. 'Come and see this dog in a jumper instead.'

'Woof!' Lucia said to Alphonse, who gave her a suspicious look.

The doorbell went again and all the other guests arrived at once. Art walked in, wearing his normal clothes, but Dee Dee had dressed in a red velvet dress with white fur trimmings like Father – or perhaps I should say Mother – Christmas, and was carrying a pile of presents. PC Green and a pregnant Dolores were wearing matching Christmas jumpers and holding more presents.

Violet ushered them all into the room. Benedict handed round glasses of mulled wine to the grown-ups and a delicious fruit punch for Art and Violet. Everybody was just saying cheers to each other when the doorbell rang again.

'I wonder who that can be?' Camille said, puzzled.

'Carol singers?' PC Green said.

Dee Dee said, 'How lovely!' and Benedict said, 'How annoying!' at exactly the same time.

'I'll go and see,' Violet said. She went into the hall and opened the door.

And there, looking rather tired and sunburnt,

was Violet's godmother, Celeste. As ever, she was clutching her camera, a backpack and a bottle of champagne.

'Violet!' she cried. 'You've grown so much since I last saw you. I finished photographing the snow leopards in the Himalayas early so I thought I must come and see you all!'

Violet grinned. 'Come in! Everyone is going to be SO pleased to see you!'

And, sure enough, Camille shrieked with delight when she saw her friend, nearly dropping a plate of mince pies.

Bring!! The doorbell rang again.

Violet went to answer it, thinking that this time it really must be carol singers, but, when she opened the door, there, standing with a pile of suitcases, was Rose.

'Surprise!' she cried, hugging Violet. 'My mother got the date wrong as usual so I came back from Paris on my own. I really wanted to see you so I've come straight from the station.'

'You're just in time for the party! Come in!' Violet cried.

Rose came through to the sitting room with Violet and everyone cheered.

'I think that calls for a toast,' PC Green said, handing Rose a glass of fruit punch.

'I agree,' Violet said, clinking her glass with everyone. 'To all our past and future adventures and, most importantly, Happy Christmas, everyone!'

Violet's extra-helpful word glossary

Violet loves words, especially if they sound unusual, so some of the words used in her story might have been a little tricky to understand. Most of them you probably know, but Violet has picked out a few to explain . . .

Sociable – Means friendly.

Sanctuary – Generally means a safe place and for animals is a place a bit like a zoo.

Eccentric – Means a bit strange but in a good way.

Con artist – Is a bad person who tricks other people into believing something that isn't true and usually takes their money.

Consulting = Means looking at.

A scholarship = Is like a prize you are given for being particularly good at something which usually means that you get given money too or don't pay any fees at a private school.

Prima ballerina = The main ballet dancer in a company.

Departure = means leaving.

Light pollution = Means when all the lights from a city or town shine up into the sky at night so you can't see the stars.

Careered = Means moved fast.

Extinct = Means no longer exists.

Crucial – Means important.

Smirked – Means smiled in a mean way.

Marriage licence – Is a certificate that you need to get before getting married.

Incognito – Means undercover or in disguise.

Riff-raff – Is a rude thing to call someone.

Emergency generator – Is a machine that turns and makes electricity if your normal supply goes off.

Emphatically – Means definitely.

Arrivederci – Means goodbye in Italian.

ACKNOWLEDGEMENTS

I have had a lot of fun writing the Violet books and, since this is the last book in the series, I thought a few thank yous were in order. First of all thank you to the amazing Becka Moor, for illustrating the books so beautifully. And then to my wonderful agent, Catherine Pellegrino, for being Violet's first supporter. Lastly a huge thank you to the brilliant team at Simon & Schuster, who have been a great pleasure to work with, and have done such a fantastic job, particularly my editor, Jane Griffiths, Mattie Whitehead, Jenny Richards, Jenny Glencross, Jane Buckley, Stephanie Purcell and the whole Rights team, and Hannah Cooper.

HAVE YOU SOLVED THE OTHER VIOLET MYSTERIES?

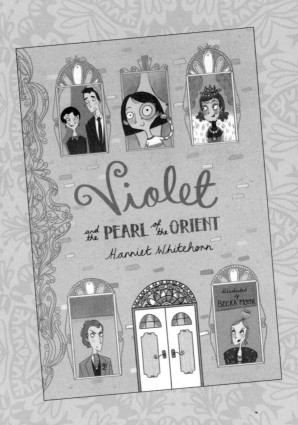

Violet
and the PEARL of the ORIENT

Harriet Whitehorn

Illustrated by
BECKA MOOR

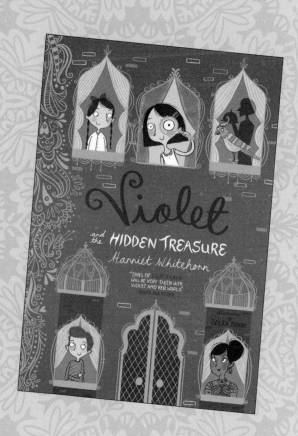

Violet
and the HIDDEN TREASURE

Harriet Whitehorn

"FANS OF ... WILL BE VERY TAKEN WITH VIOLET AND HER WORLD"
BOOKS FOR KEEPS

Illustrated by
BECKA MOOR